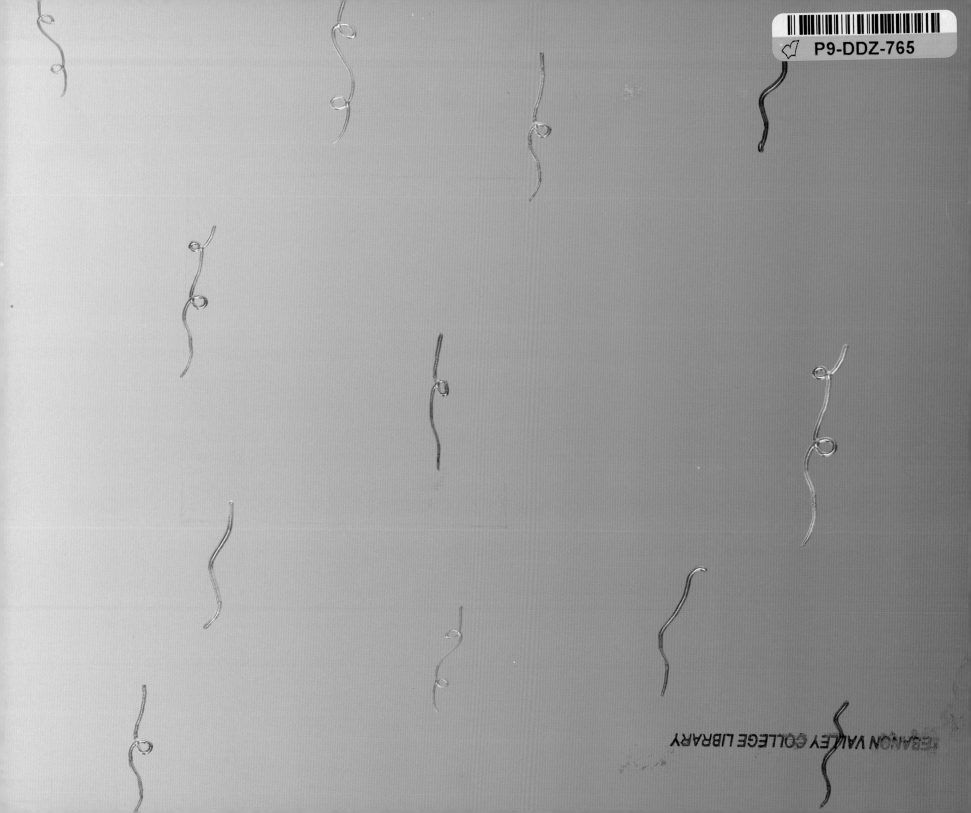

I ran to tell my family what had happened.

But most of all . . .

. . . I ran to tell them that I loved them.

Then, with a sudden bump,

I felt as though I had landed on something soft and familiar.

The white cloud faded away, as did the silver strings in my hand.

I found myself back in my bedroom, sitting on my bed!

I was home again.

. . . only white everywhere I looked.

We floated for some time,

until we came upon a huge, white cloud.

Everything around me turned as white as a blank piece of paper.

I could no longer see the stars or the moon . . .

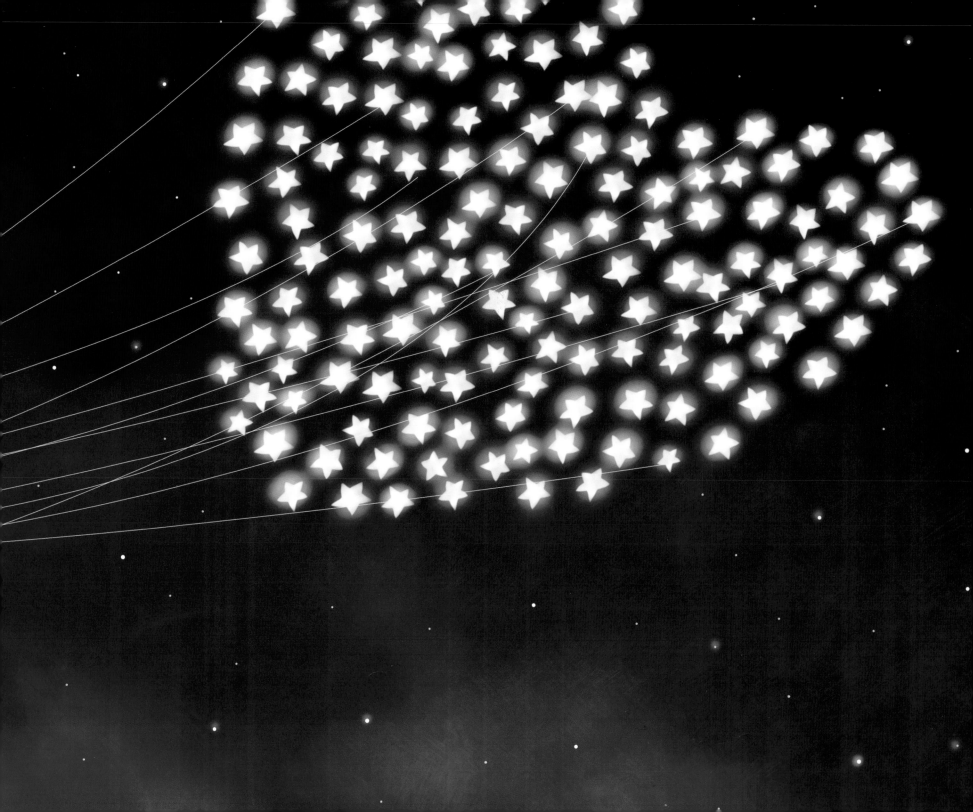

I grabbed onto the ends of the strings,

and suddenly I was lifted up and away from my island.

We began to float into the dark blue sky.

It was beautiful.

As the stars danced, the silvery strings,

which lay in a pile next to me,

began to rise up into the sky.

I watched in amazement

as each of the strings attached to a star

and floated above my hand.

The birds played and chirped overhead.

But I was too sad to enjoy their show.

I didn't even notice that the day had turned into night.

As the last bird flew by, I finally looked up to see the stars.

But tonight the stars were different.

They danced a new dance—

one I had not seen before.

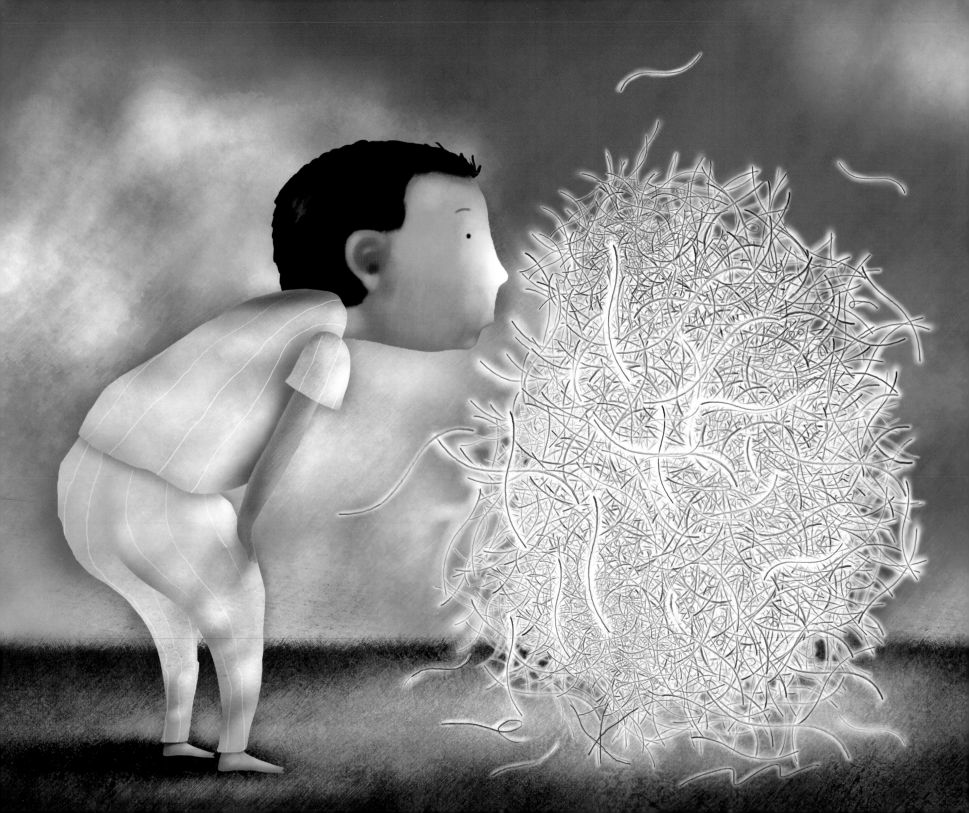

A little later, more birds flew by.

Each dropped a piece of silvery string onto my island.

Soon there lay a pile of string almost as big as I was.

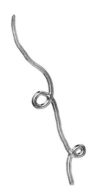

I thought that perhaps I could tie them together

to make a long rope and then climb it back home.

But I did not know which way to climb the rope—

up or down, or side to side.

How was I ever going to get back home?

My sadness turned to sorrow.

I didn't mean it when I told my family that I no longer loved them.

I didn't mean it when I told them that I wanted to always be alone.

One morning, the birds that visited each day came by

and started dropping little pieces of shiny, silvery string all around me.

I caught one to look at, but it was not very long,

so I let it fall to the ground.

I felt very sad.

The moon and stars and planets did their dance for me,

but without my family to share it with,

I no longer enjoyed their show.

During the day, the sun kept me warm

and the birds flew by to say hello,

but without anyone to share it with,

it didn't seem as special.

I missed my family very, very much.

I sat on my island, all alone, for what seemed like a long time.

I saw many moons rise and many suns set.

Although I enjoyed being alone,

after a while I began to miss my family.

I missed my mother's kisses and my father's hugs.

I even missed my little sister.

But as I looked around,

it seemed as though there was no way

to get back home.

The nighttime sky began to glow.

Its purple color started turning a warm blue,

and the dancing stars became beautiful white birds

that welcomed me to a new day.

I watched as the moon rose into the sky

and I laughed as stars and planets danced all around me.

I had never been so close to the heavens.

Saturn floated by and was so near

that I thought I could reach out and touch its rings.

I stood proudly on my new island.

It felt as though I was on top of the world.

No one to bother me,

no one to tell me what to do,

and no one to hurt my feelings.

Just me, my island, and the sky.

It was beautiful.

I was alone. My wish had come true!

When I awoke, I was lying down on a patch of cool grass.

All I could see around me was an endless blue sky.

After I stood up, I realized I was now on a very small island.

Even more surprising was that the little island was floating
in the middle of the sky.

The Planet Saturn

Once when I was a little child, I was very angry at my family.

I told them that I didn't love them.

I told them that I wished I never had a family

and could always be alone.

I ran into my room and I fell fast asleep on my bed.

Dedicated to my children,
Dylan and Chelsea

Publisher's Cataloging-in-Publication

Cutler, Dave.
    When I wished I was alone / written and illustrated by Dave Cutler.
    p. cm.
    SUMMARY: A boy who is frequently angry gets his wish when he wakes up
all alone on an island in the sky, but after a while he wishes he could go home.
    Audience: Ages 2–8
    LCCN 2003103197
    ISBN 0–9671851–0–6

    1. Anger—Juvenile fiction. 2. Anger—Fiction. I. Title

PZ7.C9778Wh 2003   [E]
                              QBI33-1263

10 9 8 7 6 5 4 3 2 1

Book design by Mulberry Tree Press, Inc. (www.mulberrytreepress.com)
Printed in Singapore.

When I Wished I Was Alone

Written and Illustrated by

Dave Cutler

GreyCore KIDS

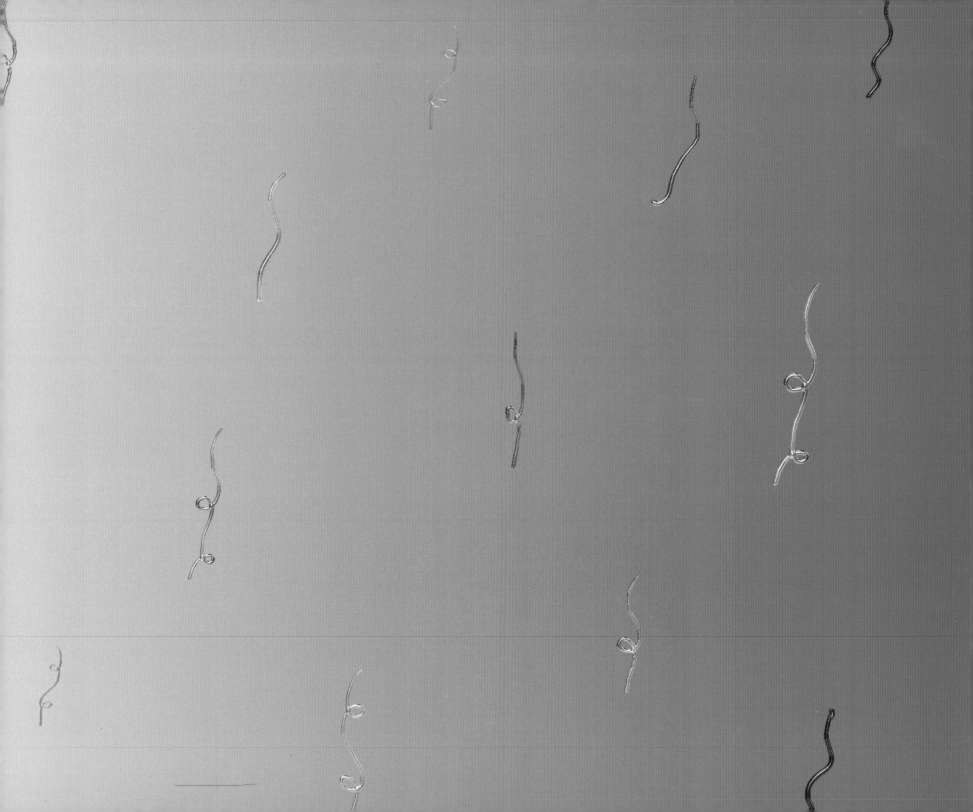